AN ALLIGATOR DAY

By Eleanor Wasmuth

Publishers • GROSSET & DUNLAP • New York

Library of Congress Catalog Card Number: 82-083743. ISBN: 0-448-21703-1.
 Published simultaneously in Canada. Printed in the United States of America.

One morning Alice and Andy said,
“We don’t know what to do today.”
“One of you could wash the
breakfast dishes,” said Mother.

“And one of you could dry the
breakfast dishes.”
“That’s no fun,” said Alice.
“I don’t want to do that.”

"You could clean up your room,"
said Mother.
"That's no fun," said Andy.
"I don't want to do that."
"Then go outside and play," Mother said.

Alice and Andy went outside.
"What do you want to do?" Andy asked.
"I don't know," said Alice.
"There is Ralph Duck," said Andy.
"Let's ask him."

"Hello, Ralph," said Alice and Andy.
"We don't know what to do today."
"Come with me," said Ralph.
"I'll give you a ride on my train."

Andy and Alice went with Ralph to
the train yard.
"All aboard," Ralph called.

Ralph took the train all around the town.
"Thank you, Ralph," said Alice and Andy.

"Look! There is Ned Squirrel.
We are going to say hello to him."

"Come for a ride in my hot
air balloon," said Ned.
"We'll have some fun in the sky."

Up, up they went.
The balloon flew up over the treetops.

"I like flying in a hot air balloon,"
said Alice.
"Look down there," said Andy.
"I see Bucky Beaver in his houseboat."
Down, down they went.

“Goodbye, Ned,” Alice and Andy said.
“Thank you for the ride.
We had a very good time!”

"Yoo hoo, Bucky," called Andy.
"Can we ride on your houseboat?"

"Sure," said Bucky.
Alice and Andy climbed aboard.

Bucky Beaver took his houseboat up the river and down the river.

"What fun, Bucky," said the two little alligators.

Just then Annabelle Rabbit came by
on her skateboard.

She showed Alice and Andy a few
skateboard tricks.

“Can we try?” asked Alice and Andy.
“Sure,” said Annabelle. “Take turns.”
Alice went first.

Wheeee, down the hill she went.

Then Andy had his turn.
Wheeee, down the hill he went.

“Thank you, Annabelle,”
Alice and Andy said.
“We’ll see you later.”

Alice and Andy went home.
"What did you two do today?" Mother asked.
"Nothing," said Alice and Andy.

“Where did you go?” Mother asked.
“No place,” said Alice and Andy.